Dedicado a todos los niños, de todas partes,
que hayan hecho un viaje como este...
y a todos los que fueron amables con ellos
a lo largo del camino.

Dedicated to all the children, everywhere,
who have made the journey . . .
and to everyone who showed them kindness
along the way

2021 First US edition
Spanish text copyright © 2021 Charlesbridge; translated by Carlos E. Calvo
Text copyright © 2020 by Hollis Kurman
Illustrations copyright © 2020 by Barroux
All rights reserved, including the right of reproduction in whole or in part
in any form. Charlesbridge and colophon are registered trademarks of
Charlesbridge Publishing, Inc.

At the time of publication, all URLs printed in this book were accurate and active.
Charlesbridge, the author, and the illustrator are not responsible for the content
or accessibility of any website.

Published by Charlesbridge
9 Galen Street, Watertown, MA 02472
(617) 926-0329 · www.charlesbridge.com

First published in Great Britain in 2020 by Otter-Barry Books, Little Orchard,
Burley Gate, Hereford, HR1 3QS, as *Hello! A Counting Book of Kindnesses*

Printed in China
(hc) 10 9 8 7 6 5 4 3 2 1

Library of Congress Cataloging-In-Publication data
available upon request

Illustrations done in watercolor
Display type set in Mr. Dodo by Hipopotam Studio
Text type set in Supernett Condensed by FaceType
Color separations by XY Digital
Printed by Toppan Leefung, Dongguan, China
Production supervision by Gill Woolcott
Designed by Jon Simeon

A Contar amabilidad
Counting Kindness

Diez formas de darles la bienvenida a niños refugiados
Ten Ways to Welcome Refugee Children

HOLLIS KURMAN   Ilustrado por / Illustrated by BARROUX   Traducido por / Translated by CARLOS E. CALVO

Charlesbridge

Cuando el lugar donde vivimos
nos da tanto miedo que
tenemos que irnos, todo gesto
de amabilidad es importante.

When a place gets so scary
that we have to leave home,
every kindness counts.

1

Un barco

nos ayuda a hacer el viaje.

One boat

helping us on our way.

2
Dos manos
nos alzan para estar a salvo.

Two hands
lifting us to safety.

3
Tres comidas
nos llenan la barriga.

Three meals
filling us up.

4

Cuatro camas
nos mantienen seguros y calentitos.

Four beds
keeping us safe and warm.

5
Cinco deseos
nos dan esperanza y fuerza.

Five wishes
giving us hope and strength.

6
Seis libros
nos cuentan historias
nuevas con palabras nuevas.

Six books
sharing new stories and words.

7
Siete días
celebrando nuestra primera
semana en un nuevo país.

Seven days
celebrating our first week
in a new land.

LUNES
MONDAY

MARTES
TUESDAY

MIÉRCOLES
WEDNESDAY

8
Ocho regalos
nos sorprenden con cosas que nos gustan y que necesitamos.

Eight gifts
surprising us with things we like and need.

9

Nueve corazones
nos dan la bienvenida a nuestra nueva escuela.

Nine hearts
welcoming us to our new school.

10
Diez amigos
¡nos hacen sentir felices!

Ten friends

making us happy!

¿De qué otras formas se puede ayudar?
How many more ways are there to help?

BIENVENIDOS
WELCOME

1	**2**	**3**	**4**	**5**
uno	dos	tres	cuatro	cinco
one	two	three	four	five

ACERCA DE LOS NIÑOS REFUGIADOS

- Millones de niños se vieron obligados a abandonar su hogar debido a guerras, inundaciones y otros eventos terribles.

- Muchos niños refugiados fueron separados de sus padres y de sus hermanos.

- Más que la mitad de los refugiados de todo el mundo son niños (¡más de diez millones de niños!). Necesitan un lugar seguro donde vivir.

ABOUT CHILD REFUGEES

- Millions of children have been forced to leave their homes due to war, floods, or other scary events.

- Many child refugees have been separated from their parents and siblings.

- Over half of the world's refugees are children (more than ten million kids). They need a safe place to live.

GRACIAS
THANKS

6
seis
six

7
siete
seven

8
ocho
eight

9
nueve
nine

10
diez
ten

PARA AYUDAR O PARA MÁS INFORMACIÓN

TO HELP OR FIND OUT MORE

Al Otro Lado • www.alotrolado.org

Amnesty International • www.amnestyusa.org

Human Rights Watch • www.hrw.org

Save the Children • www.savethechildren.org

UNICEF • www.unicef.org

War Child • www.warchildusa.org